SILENT NIGHT

A Western Adventure

A.T. BUTLER

CHAPTER ONE

Jacob Payne, bounty hunter, pulled up the collar on his coat and smiled to himself. He had been waiting for this for months. Temperatures closer to thirty than to eighty was what December was supposed to feel like. Here in Tucson there wouldn't be too many weeks of weather this cold, not like back in Virginia, but he would enjoy it while he had the chance.

Jacob hurried down the busy dirt street through town, reveling in the piercing cold even in the middle of a sunny day. He wanted to be early for meeting Bonnie Loft as she finished her shift at the San Xavier Cafe; he reminded himself he had plenty of time to enjoy the cold weather. It should hang around for at least another couple months. He hoped. What was Christmas without a coat at the very least?

Even from a distance Jacob could tell that the cafe was crowded—strange for the middle of the afternoon. As he opened the door and crossed the threshold, though, he understood why. Coming inside from the cold, in from the outdoors, the San Xavier Cafe was a welcoming haven. Whatever Mrs. Everill had been cooking all morning had made the entire place smell of cinnamon and cloves with an undercurrent of butter. Jacob took a good, deep whiff of the spiced air as he looked around.

There wasn't an empty table in the place. Everywhere he looked, Jacob saw his friends and neighbors talking and laughing over their meals. Men that Jacob knew should be out tending to stock or repairing a roof lounged at a cafe table clutching a mug of coffee. Women that Jacob recognized as busy wives and mothers leaned their heads close together, whispering and laughing at whatever gossip they shared.

Tucson was booming. They had just gotten their first newspaper a few months prior, and word had it that Phoenix (over a hundred miles north) would soon be an incorporated city as well. The Territory of Arizona was filling up, and though Jacob had come west to give himself a fresh start away from people, he had to admit that finding himself in a place surrounded by friends and neighbors, by people he cared about, was a welcome surprise.

Mickey, the bartender, waved Jacob over from where he stood in the doorway to the cafe.

Shrugging off his coat, Jacob made his way over. He found a lone barstool in between two pairs of men, and leaned forward to be heard over the din of the room.

"What's all this, Mick?" Jacob asked. "You all giving away some free pie or something?"

"Ach, no. The few days before Christmas have been our busiest the last few years. Mrs. Everill claims it's a combination of the cold outside and folks not wanting to work if they don't have to and the general feelings of community and generosity as the holiday approaches. I've seen men get into fistfights after arguing about who was going to pay for that next round of drinks." He shook his head as Jacob laughed.

"Well, I promise not to fight anyone who wants to buy me a drink."

Micky waved him off. "You don't worry me, Payne. I know you're not staying." He pulled out his pocket watch to verify the time. "Bonnie should be out here any second and then you'll whisk her away, won't you?"

"If she wants to be whisked away I am happy to be the man to do that job," Jacob averred.

Mickey chuckled as he turned to give another patron his attention.

Jacob turned around and leaned with his back to the bar. From this spot he could watch the happenings in the cafe. Though he wasn't currently hunting down an outlaw, and didn't have any intentions to take a new job until January, he couldn't very well turn off his instincts. Jacob surveyed the room carefully, looking for suspicious behavior, for men who were trying to hide something or strangers that seemed out of place. This was what he was best at, after all. Watching. Listening. Observing. And homing in on the outlaw that was trying to evade capture.

Bonnie Loft shyly stepped into his line of view. Jacob smiled widely at her and quickly hopped down off the barstool.

"Miss Loft," he said, unnaturally formal and bowing slightly.

"Mr. Payne," she replied.

"May I escort you out of the cafe?" He offered his arm as he over-enunciated each of the words, figuring if he was going to play into the formal nature of their meeting he might as well go all the way.

It worked. She laughed and took his arm in response. He led her out of the San Xavier Cafe, not even bothering to say good-bye to Mickey.

The couple didn't speak again until they had exited the crowded building and were back in the cold, relative quiet of the street.

"You sure you don't mind doing a little shopping with me, Jacob?"

Bonnie huddled close to him against the cold and Jacob stood up a little straighter, proud to be the one to provide that protection for her.

"I can't think of a single thing I would mind doing with you," he promised her.

"I'd like to send some gifts back home to my family."

"That's very generous of you."

She shrugged, looking into the big front window of the hardware store they passed. "Family is family. I honestly don't know if I will ever see them again, so this is just a little way I can make sure they know I'm thinking about them."

Jacob was silent, thinking about his own family back in Virginia. He had sent them one telegram when he had arrived in Tucson almost a year ago, just so they would know he was alive, and know where to find him if they absolutely had to. But beyond that he hadn't had any desire to contact them again. After losing his wife and son, Jacob was more inclined to feel like he had no family at all, rather than thinking of his brothers as family.

"This is your first Christmas since leaving Virginia, isn't it?" Bonnie continued.

"Yeah, it is. But ..." He faltered, embarrassed for the first time by his distance from his family.

"Well," Bonnie said, picking up the thread and saving him from having to defend himself, "this year you can come with me to the Nativity play at my church."

"That might be nice," he agreed. "It's the night before Christmas?"

"Yes, but I promised to help with the costumes. Somehow in the next few days I need to put together outfits for the shepherds and Mary and Joseph and all." She laughed at the thought. "You'll be in town, won't you?"

"I will. I already told the marshal. I'm not planning on taking any new jobs until at least the new year. I have plenty of things to take care of around home and I don't need to be leaving the warm home fire at the holidays."

"The warm home fire of your boarding house?" she teased.

"Oh, well." He grinned. "It's an expression. I'll have a warm home fire sometime."

She smiled up at him and seemed about to say something further before turning her attention to the store on their right.

"Here we are," she announced. "Can we go in there?"

In answer, Jacob opened the door for her, ushering Bonnie into the warm interior of the Tucson General Store.

This town was growing and they were getting more and more specialized shops, but the general store, run by the Towers family for the last six years, would always be a pillar. As they entered, Jacob noticed the store was almost as crowded as San Xavier Cafe had been, mostly women with arms and baskets full of all the supplies they would need for a festive family holiday in the next few days.

"Are you here for anything specific?" he asked, looking around.

Bonnie shook her head. "I have some ideas, but it's more that I'll know it when I see it."

Jacob nodded. "You lead the way, then.

Consider me your packhorse. I am at your disposal."

Bonnie beamed at him and tugged his arm gently, leading him down a crowded aisle between shelves of cooking utensils and barrels of dry food stuffs. Though Jacob felt completely out of his element, he enjoyed his busy afternoon of shopping with Bonnie. After a thorough search, she settled on a bolt of calico fabric for her parents, along with other small things for herself and her fellow lodgers. Simple though it may be, she thought that whatever her mother made with the calico would remind them of their daughter. She worried about the cost to ship it all the way back to the east coast, but reconciled herself with the fact that she would not be going herself. She needed to send them something.

"I'm only partway through writing my letter to them," she told Jacob, as Mrs. Towers packaged up her purchases. "I want to tell them everything, and give them a lovely thick envelope to pour over."

"That's thoughtful."

"You don't think your family would like the same thing?"

Jacob thought briefly before shaking his head. He couldn't remember his brother ever reading anything other than the Bible and his account ledgers. A letter would just confound him; he would find it wasteful.

"That's not the kind of family we are," he said simply. The bounty hunter gathered up Bonnie's packages in both arms. "You'll have to lead the way." He indicated the door to the store with a nod of his head. It was far too crowded inside for them to walk side by side. "I'll walk you home."

She smiled at him again, her warm and grateful smile, and led him to the street.

CHAPTER TWO

Walking through the door of the Golden Saddle Saloon later that night, Jacob again reflected on what his life might be like with Bonnie a bigger part of it. He had been thinking about her as a partner, as his home, for the better part of a month and was beginning to feel like the time had come. It weighed constantly on him how much more would he prefer to be home with her, by his home fire, rather than coming out to the saloon for a drink and socialization.

Because, as always, this place came with a price. Sure, Jacob easily found Edwin Hogg, Lucky and Abe, but he also noticed the bounty hunter Clifford Pierce trying to get his attention from the other side of the room. Jacob and Clifford had played a memorable game of poker just the last week, all as a ploy to capture the outlaw Billy Watts. As part of that game, Watts had shot Pierce and Jacob had to hunt down the kid on his own.

In the days since, Clifford Pierce seemed to vacillate between being grateful to Jacob for the assistance and being resentful of how much he owed him. Apparently, this evening Pierce was feeling some kind of holiday spirit. Not long after Jacob walked through the door, Pierce seemed determined to get his attention and draw him over.

Jacob waved to acknowledge him, but something else caught his attention.

The Golden Saddle Saloon wasn't quite as crowded as San Xavier Cafe had been earlier in the day, but it seemed apparent that plenty of men were taking advantage of the one warm place they could gather at this time of night. Tucson was a big enough town by now to have plenty of men coming and going on their way through other places in the territory. Jacob was used to seeing strangers.

He was not, however, used to those same strangers watching him.

Jacob couldn't say what it was that caught his attention; maybe it was simply the unsettling calm emanating from that chair across from Pierce where the man sat quietly smoking. This stranger had long, straggly hair, so oily it appeared darker than it probably was. He also caught Jacob's eye and gave him a smile that seemed more menacing than friendly.

Pierce waved Jacob over, and the quiet, dirty man just watched. By this time of night, so many of the men in the saloon were deep into their third drink. The quiet ones tended to stick out a bit more.

As he stood near the bar, he tried to keep the man visible in his periphery while not letting him know he was being watched. His maneuver didn't last long, however. Clifford Pierce had evidently gotten tired of trying to get Jacob's attention and simply came to meet him at the bar.

"Payne," he said, grabbing the bounty hunter's arm. "You seem like you're a million miles away. Didn't you hear me calling for you? Maybe you just need a drink."

Pierce signaled for the bartender, and Jacob noticed how slowly and stiffly he was moving. Being shot in the gut will do that to a man, he supposed. Pierce seemed to struggle to raise a hand above his shoulder, grimacing as he tried.

"I'm fine, Cliff," Jacob said, putting his own hand up. "I'll get one."

"You get your drink then you come over to my table." He indicated over his shoulder. "I got a story to tell you."

Jacob raised his eyebrows questioningly.

"Yep," Pierce said. "Saw the marshal this afternoon. You'll never guess who's sitting in jail right now."

"All right," Jacob said. Though he wasn't particularly fond of Clifford Pierce, he was never one to say no to a story, especially one that might inadvertently provide him with a clue he needed for a future case. U.S. Marshal Owen Santos had never been careless with his words. Jacob wanted to know what Pierce knew.

Plus that mystery man seemed to raise more questions in Jacob than answers. Maybe he could satisfy his curiosity by joining their table.

Jacob watched Pierce make his way back to the table, where two other men sat waiting for him: the stranger and one of Tucson's deputies. The other bounty hunter took an empty chair from the table next to him; from this distance it seemed as though he got into some altercation with the men there, but Jacob couldn't hear anything.

Instead, he turned his attention to Pete Pendleton, the bartender who had just found a moment in between serving the other patrons to wait on Jacob.

"Beer, Payne?" he asked.

Jacob nodded. "Make it two. Save me a trip back up here."

Pete laughed. "Glad to hear you'll be staying a while. I'll get those right away for you."

A couple minutes later, with a glass in each hand, Jacob followed the same path he had watched Pierce take to the small table near the front of the saloon. The quiet smoking man that had caught Jacob's eye earlier continued to watch him, though Jacob didn't meet his eye.

"Payne," Pierce exclaimed when he saw him. "It's about time. Come. Sit."

Nodding to the other two men, he sat at Pierce's left side. "How's that hole in your torso, Pierce?"

The other bounty hunter frowned briefly before waving off the question. "Fine fine. It'll heal. Don't you worry about me. Give me another couple weeks and I'll again be riding the trail right alongside you."

"We'll see about that."

"You know Deputy Little, don't you? What about Andrew Coleman? He ain't been in Tucson long." Pierce gestured to the other two men who tipped their hats.

Jacob nodded to each of them in turn. "Deputy. Mr. Coleman. Pleasure to meet you."

Coleman tucked a piece of dirty hair behind his ear and stayed silent.

"The deputy was there when Santos was telling me. Yeah, so apparently this afternoon, only a few hours ago, he arrested Ben Wilbourne."

Jacob had only been half listening to Pierce until he heard the name. "Wilbourne? Isn't he the kid that the Towers family brought with them from back east? The little black child?"

"I don't know that I'd call him a child, myself. That boy must be at least fifteen now, but yes, you're thinking of the right man. He stole a couple hundred dollars from the telegraph office, they say."

Jacob paused in bringing his glass to his lips. "How is that possible?"

Jacob hadn't ever had an interaction with the young man, but every time he had had reason to go into the general store, Ben was on hand. Usually, Mr. Towers tasked him with cleaning or carrying stock, but at least once Jacob saw him following a family back to their home, his arms laden with their purchases. He had seemed such a gentle, trust-worthy boy. Mr. Towers wouldn't stand for anything less.

"How?" he said again. "Did he confess? What is this arrest based on?"

"They found the remains of a cigarette and a button at the scene of the crime."

"That's not— Are we're sure that was his button? Did anyone see Wilbourne?"

Pierce shrugged. "Not that I know of. But, you know, Payne. Some people just aren't trustworthy. Wilbourne works— *worked* at the general store where he could get any number of buttons. He probably stole from them too and then accidentally dropped one when he was rushing away from the scene of the crime."

Jacob shook his head. "That's ridiculous. I don't understand how Santos can be okay with that. Seems like awfully little to be making an arrest on."

"I don't know what to tell you. This is all what I heard straight from the marshal."

Jacob downed his beer and stood.

"It was a pleasure to meet you, boys. But this news has made me think. I'm gonna go see the marshal for myself."

"He ain't there now, Payne. Stay. Have a seat. Have another drink. It won't do you no good to go now. The boy will still be arrested in the morning and you can talk to the marshal then."

Still standing, Jacob looked from Pierce to

the door and back again. He hated to admit that the other bounty hunter was right. There wasn't anything he could do right now.

"Well. All right. I did promise Bonnie I wouldn't go chasing outlaws for a bit yet anyway."

"See? There you go," Pierce said, nodding.

"Let me go grab another beer and I'll be back."

The bar was even more crowded than it had been previously, and Jacob had a difficult time getting Pete's attention. By the time he had made it back to the table, his seat had been taken by Deputy Lowry. All the other men were deep in conversation.

"Well now, Mr. Coleman," Jacob said, standing over the table. "You only been in town a short while? What brings you to Tucson?"

"You really hadn't met him yet?" Pierce asked, surprised. "I thought for sure I told you about him. He came along as a second for me when I went after that road bandit a few weeks ago. He's a great shot. Good man."

"Nice to meet you," Jacob said.

Coleman took the cigarette out of his mouth and grinned at Jacob. He was missing one of his eyeteeth, the dark hole making his smile off balance. Nevertheless, he seemed nice enough, and though Jacob didn't exactly love Pierce, he knew him to be a decent man who wouldn't be associating with someone dangerous.

Jacob wasn't sure what to make of the fact that Coleman had been watching him so closely that evening, but he supposed maybe it was his imagination. He looked back up across the room where Ed Hogg had been waving for his attention for the last ten minutes.

"Well, Pierce, it's been nice catching up, but I got a couple guys in the back there that have been trying to get my attention all night. Think I'll go make an appearance."

CHAPTER THREE

Jacob woke up the next morning with a long list of things he needed to do. With Christmas a few days away, there was only so much time to get all the chores and errands done that needed doing. He had told his landlady that he'd take care of killing the goose for her, for example. That would be a project itself.

And then after hearing the details about Ben Wilbourne's arrest from Pierce, Jacob had a nagging feeling something was off about that. He couldn't say what, but digging into that case a bit more got moved to the top of his list of things to do.

He tried to tell himself it was none of his business, that the marshal had everything under control and the boy surely could handle his self.

But that persistent feeling of unease stuck with him all night. It distracted him enough during his poker game with Ed the night before, that his friend flat out refused to play with him anymore after taking too much of his money.

And now, in the bright light of a December morning, Jacob knew he would need to at least go inquire about the boy or he'd never have any rest. He had plans to meet Bonnie for dinner, so wanted to get his own distractions taken care of before then.

After knocking on the door to the marshal's office, Jacob let himself in. He was surprised to see that the marshal was not alone this early in the morning.

Pastor Ambrose's face lit up at the sight of Jacob walking through the door.

"Pastor," he said. "I'm sorry. I don't want to interrupt."

"No, no, Payne," the marshal said, standing to greet him. "Pastor Ambrose is here to talk to our prisoner. You're not interrupting anything."

"Yes, I had heard something about that," Jacob said. "Pierce told me."

Marshal Santos rolled his eyes as the pastor laughed.

"I should have guessed. That man runs his mouth more than my wife does."

"Well, he's only hurting himself, isn't he?" the pastor pointed out. "Can't be good for his business if he gets the reputation for being a talker."

"That's true," Jacob said. "That's why I never say a dang thing."

This time the marshal laughed. "And that's why you're here, is it, Payne? To just stand quietly in the corner?"

"All right. I get it. I'm guilty. I admit I have some questions for you."

"Of course. Let me just take the pastor here back and I'll be right with you."

The two men left Jacob alone in the office as they headed back to where the small collection of jail cells waited. Listening hard, Jacob determined that the cells seemed to be mostly full. That made sense as it had been several weeks since the circuit judge had been around these parts. They were expecting him back any day, and all these prisoners would have to stand trial.

Jacob was seated where the pastor had been, in the chair in front of the desk, when the marshal returned.

"What can I do for you, Payne? I got a stack of wanted bulletins over there, but I thought you told me you weren't interested till after the holidays."

"I did. I'm not. I just ... Truthfully, Marshal, I'm not rightly sure what I'm doing here. I spoke to Clifford Pierce last night and he told me about a boy that has been arrested and something about his story didn't sit right with me."

"A boy?" The marshal frowned. "Well, the youngest man I got in here is Benjamin Wilbourne who robbed the telegraph office. But he's not any boy. He's fifteen. That's plenty old to be held accountable for his actions."

"You're right. That's true." Jacob hesitated, unsure of how to proceed. He had never directly challenged the marshal before.

"So, tell me what Pierce said that's got you so worried, then."

"Well." He cleared his throat. "I understand that you found a button and a cigarette butt at the scene of the robbery."

"That's right."

"And did anyone see Benjamin or ... did you find the cash that he stole?"

"Not yet. I aim to go over to the general store to look through his things later today."

Jacob hesitated only a moment before volunteering. "I'll help, if you like."

The marshal narrowed his eyes at him, scrutinizing. "What's your angle, Payne? I didn't expect to see you at all for another week and now you're volunteering to investigate a case that's already solved?"

"I just ... Well, there's something about all of this that doesn't sit right with me. I'm worried that we may have the wrong man. Everything I know about Benjamin Wilbourne tells me he never would have done something like this."

"You don't trust me, Payne?" the marshal said. While his words were simply inquiring, his tone was hard. Jacob could tell that he had struck a nerve in the other man.

"It's not that, Marshal. I mean no disrespect. Call it a gut feeling, if you want, but something about this doesn't seem right. I hope I'm wrong. I hope it was just my bias against Pierce that makes me feel like he was spouting nonsense. But I can't focus on anything else until I at least have a look."

The marshal clenched his jaw, and turned away. There were a few shelves lining the wall behind his desk, and Jacob watched him cross and pick up a small animal skull absentmindedly before setting it down again.

"You know I ought to have you horse-whipped for even suggesting that the wrong man is behind bars, don't you?"

"I'm not doing that, Marshal. My apologies if it seems like—"

"You *are* doing that. I've known you how long now? A year? In all that time, in all the men we've captured together, you've never once given me trouble. But now, you hear about the case secondhand and assume because you didn't capture the man yourself that the wrong man is behind bars."

"Marshal, I swear—"

"I wouldn't have thought it of you, Payne. In all this time we've never once come close to disagreeing. But now you gotta pull this stunt right at the holidays."

Jacob kept his mouth shut this time; he had learned that there wasn't any use arguing with the marshal. He could have Jacob thrown in one of those cells himself.

The marshal sighed, still eyeing the bounty hunter critically.

"I don't like this. You know that. I don't like it one bit, but ... Well, I'd be a poor marshal if I didn't trust the men I know to be good ones. I'm going to indulge you."

Jacob let out the breath he had been holding. "Thank you."

"It might just be giving you enough rope to hang yourself, but ..." He shrugged. "I believe that you want to be wrong and you'll do the right thing. Just know"—he pointed his finger in Jacob's face—"I don't intend to help you a whit. This is your problem to solve, if in fact there is a problem."

"I understand. Can I talk to him?"

"As soon as the pastor is done in there. Wilbourne asked for him as soon as I came in this morning. I'm hoping he's making a confession we can use. The judge is supposed to be here soon and the more evidence I have to convict the better."

Jacob nodded. Just a couple days. That's all the time he had to find out what he needed to find out. And a good chunk of that time was already spoken for; he wasn't about to cancel plans with Bonnie Loft for a potential wild goose chase like this.

"You won't regret it, Marshal. I promise I just want to ease my own mind a bit. I expect to be wrong."

Marshal Santos snorted in disbelief. "When's the last time you were wrong?"

CHAPTER FOUR

Fifteen minutes later, Marshal Owen Santos had escorted Jacob back to the jail cell of Benjamin Wilbourne and closed the door behind him. When the heavy metal latch snapped shut, Jacob took a deep breath and a long, focused look at the man sitting on the cot in front of him.

Though Jacob knew Benjamin was perfectly capable and mature enough, he had a hard time looking at him and considering him a man. He had a round, baby-ish face, with no evidence of a razor having ever touched him. Though tall, Benjamin was thin as a rail. He didn't seem particularly malnourished; it was more that his body seemed to go through all the food he could feed it. His muscles were still forming.

Benjamin Wilbourne had all the evidence of a boy still about him, still growing, still trying to find his place in the world.

"Hello," Jacob said gently.

The boy sat on the cot, feet pulled up with his arms wrapped around his knees.

"Do you know who I am?"

The boy shook his head. He had not taken his eyes off of Jacob since the latter entered the cell.

"My name is Jacob Payne. I'm a bounty hunter. My job is to find the criminals who are wanted to meet justice for their crimes."

Benjamin blanched. Though obviously of a darker complexion than many of the other citizens of Tucson, his skin was a medium brown, and light enough that Jacob could notice him paling at the mention of being a criminal.

"I've been told a little bit about why you're in here. Do you want to tell me about it?"

Benjamin shook his head before burying his face in his arms.

Jacob didn't know what to do. Maybe this boy was guilty. Or maybe he was just scared.

"Look ..." Jacob said. He had been standing over the boy. "Can I sit?"

Without looking at him, Benjamin scooted

over to one side of the cot, leaving enough room for at least a foot of space between them.

"Look," Jacob said again. "I want to help you if I can. If you did this crime, I can see about getting you a lawyer for when the judge—"

"I didn't."

"What?"

"I didn't do it."

Jacob put his hand on the boy's arm, prompting him to look up. "Tell me. I can't help you if you don't tell me."

At that, Benjamin's eyes filled with tears. Jacob had never been comfortable at the sight of other men crying, but somehow this boy in his fear and his agitation was worse.

"Let's start at the beginning," Jacob suggested. "How long have you been in Tucson?"

Benjamin wiped away his tear, nodding and sitting up straight. "Okay. All right. You ... You're sure you can help me, sir?"

"I'll do my best."

"Okay. I ... I came out west with the Towers family when I was a real little kid. My family had all been owned by their family for years and years, but after the war ..."

"It's okay," Jacob said gently. "You can tell me. No one is going to get in trouble."

"My family," he began quietly. "They all just ... My pa escaped to fight for the north and my ma died and my brothers all ... they were just gone. Some sold, some escaped, some ... failed at escaping, I think. I never did find out what happened to them. I was maybe ten or so when we was freed, but I didn't have anywhere to go. I suppose I could leave now, but I was too scared then. I been with the Towers family my whole life. They gave me a place."

"I'm sure you all did what you thought best." Jacob tried to reassure him. "No point in wishing for a different outcome now."

He nodded. "Ever since we got out here I've been trying to do my share. There's always plenty of work to do around here, especially when the kids went off to school. I was the only extra pair of hands for Mr. Towers as we were building the store and getting it going. I remember entire days spent outdoors, swinging that hammer when we first got here."

He trailed off, as though he were miles and years away in his memory. Jacob didn't want to interrupt him, afraid to derail what might be a confession of guilt.

After a moment, Benjamin began again. "I know they're not really my family. I'm not stupid. I know that they were just being good

Christians by taking care of a little orphaned, homeless black boy and that I could be thrown out on my own at any time.

"I guess that's what happened now, isn't it? I should have expected it. I should have prepared better for this possibility."

"What would you be doing now if you weren't in this prison cell?"

"Lots of things. I'm fifteen. Lots of boys my age go out on their own, don't they? I've been loyal to the Towers family, but I could be making my own way soon. Mr. Towers didn't pay me a salary, but ... I could have been saving all the gifts and tips that I've gotten over the years, to be more ready."

"You don't have any money at all?" Jacob watched him carefully for evidence of hiding or lying.

"I think maybe three or four dollars." He looked up at Jacob for validation of some kind.

Jacob weighed his next words carefully. "You know why you're in here, Benjamin?"

"Yes, sir. I do. I know that ..." He paused and collected himself. "The marshal tells me that I was seen leaving the telegraph office by a lady who has a store nearby and that some money was stole from there. But, I didn't do it. I didn't take anything. I was there—I was dropping off an order from the store for Mr. Wood to take home to his wife. But I didn't take anything. I'm not a thief, sir. I would never do that."

"It's not just that you were seen, Benjamin. It's that they found a couple things in the office that point to you."

The boy frowned, puzzled.

"The marshal didn't tell you about this?" Jacob asked.

"Huh-uh. No, sir. No, I didn't hear nothing about anything they found. What could it be? I don't have anything."

Jacob narrowed his eyes, watching him. "Well, you have something. You have the clothes on your back. You have the food that Mr. Towers gives you. Do you smoke, by chance? Do you play cards? Ride a horse? Benjamin, in the eyes of the law ... anything you touch has the potential to be a piece of evidence leading back to you. You don't have to be a rich rancher to have enough to be a clue."

"But— But, I didn't do it, sir."

He sounded desperate now. Jacob wondered how the conversation with Pastor Ambrose had gone. This boy seemed to be defiant about his situation.

"Well ..." He took a deep breath. Jacob had

to weigh his conscience—going against what the marshal had said and done, versus doing what he could to find out the truth for this boy. The bounty hunter had met plenty of hardened criminals, he had seen dozens, if not hundreds of men lying and obfuscating and doing everything they could to avoid having to meet their justice.

Benjamin Wilbourne didn't display any of those signals that Jacob was used to looking for.

"Look at me."

The kid pulled his head up reluctantly from where it had been resting between his knees. He looked at Jacob, but cautiously, timidly, like a dog that had been beat one too many times and didn't really believe that he was free of that trap.

"Benjamin, I want to believe you," Jacob said finally. "I'm going to try to believe you, and I'm going to look for the evidence that could possibly get you out of here."

The boy's eyes lit up, but Jacob felt compelled to quench them immediately.

"I'm not promising anything. You have to understand that. You'll stay in this cell until I can find the real guilty party or until the judge comes to Tucson and pronounces sentence. I may fail, but I want you to know that I'll try."

"Thank you, sir," he whispered.

"Don't thank me yet," Jacob said. "Now, let's start at the beginning. Tell me everything you did on that day. Everyone you spoke to, everyone you saw, everything you touched. Even if you think it's unimportant, you need to tell me."

Benjamin nodded, and began.

CHAPTER FIVE

Jacob left the cell after more than an hour of talking over the entire case with Benjamin. The poor kid knew almost nothing about the actual details of his own case. He had to call for Marshal Santos to let him out, which meant also suffering under the other man's glares and muttering under his breath.

When they got back out to the office, Jacob tried to smooth things over.

"Marshal, I'm sorry—"

"Don't, Jacob." He held up a hand to forestall any protests as he collapsed into his office chair. "I already told you. I trust you. I'm not happy about this, but I trust your instinct and as long as you don't interfere with what I already have going on I'm not going to stop you doing a little poking around on your own."

"Thank you." Jacob sat in the chair across from the marshal's desk.

"But you need to know what you're up against. If the judge finds him guilty, Benjamin could be put to death."

Jacob frowned. Though he suspected that to be the case, hearing it said out loud made him feel like he had a pit in his stomach. His gut told him that kid was innocent but he didn't know how to prove it with all the evidence, meager though it was, pointing in the other direction.

Regardless of how this all played out, though, Jacob didn't want to take up any more of the marshal's time. It was in his best interest to keep on the man's good side as much as possible.

"I hear you," Jacob said. "I know you don't want an innocent man punished anymore that I do. I'll do my best, for Benjamin and for the law."

"You do that," the marshal said. "Now, if you don't mind," he pointed at his desk, "I have a lot of work to do. I trust you can see yourself out."

Jacob winced to himself at the coldness in the lawman's voice, but did as he said.

Once he got out onto the street, Jacob realized he didn't have much time before he was supposed to meet Bonnie. Somehow in their conversation the day before, she had contrived to get him to volunteer to help with the church Nativity play.

Benjamin was counting on him.

But so was Bonnie.

Jacob would figure out a way to help both of them.

In the meantime, however, he had an appointment to keep. Jacob had just enough time to walk the several blocks through Tucson to the Everlasting Hope Church, where he would be assigned with helping to build a set for the upcoming pageant. It had been more than a year since he had built anything even remotely similar, but he was willing to try.

Just as when he visited the church for Sunday services, when Jacob approached the church the double front doors were thrown open wide. He cautiously stepped over the threshold. He couldn't remember the last time he had visited a church not on Sunday. There was something about being in this building at another time of day that made the experience feel not quite real.

"Jacob!" a voice called from the front of the sanctuary.

As Jacob's eyes adjusted to the dimmer light indoors, he noticed that Pastor Ambrose was standing in a knot of several parishioners at the front of the church. One of them, a woman with dark hair, also waved to him to come join them. Jacob strode down the center aisle of the church toward Bonnie, two other women, the pastor and another man. It appeared as though Jacob had interrupted some kind of discussion.

"You came!" Bonnie rushed up to meet him, smiling up at him with an open, grateful expression.

"Of course I came," Jacob said, frowning a little that she had expected otherwise. "I'm not late, am I?"

"It's just that ... Well, Pastor Ambrose said he had run into you at the jail this morning, so I wasn't sure if you were going to be busy doing something else."

Jacob felt a stab of guilt at her assumption. She hadn't said it unkindly or blaming in any way, but it was apparent that she didn't truly believe that he would be there for her. That was one thing he loved about Bonnie—that she was always so understanding about his job. But it was also the one thing he hated to ask of her again and again.

"Yes, he did but ... well, the reason I was at the jail isn't going to get in the way of the promises I've made to you. Don't you worry. I'm here to help."

"I'm so glad," she said, grabbing his hand. "Come along. The pastor was just telling us what still needs to be done before tomorrow night."

Half an hour later, Jacob had been put to work building a rough manger for the baby Jesus to lay in. Bonnie and Mrs. Cicero had to explain to him how big he needed to make it—newborn baby Jesus would be played by the ten-month-old Morehead boy—but once he got started, it was a relatively easy project. As he went about cutting and nailing the wood pieces needed to create the youngster's temporary bed, Bonnie had been tasked with starting the robes for the shepherds. She was able to sit near where Jacob was working as she cut out the fabric from the pattern.

As none of the other churchgoers were nearby, Jacob took the chance of being alone with Bonnie to explain to her why he was at the jail and what he aimed to do over the next day.

"So, there's a chance this poor boy didn't steal anything at all and is just sitting in that jail cell for someone else's crime?"

"That's right. And I want to help the poor kid, but I'm not sure I can find the right evidence to negate what the marshal has already found."

"What are you going to do?"

"I don't know," he admitted. "Benjamin told me everything he did that day, but ... I don't have a single thing that tells me whether or not he's telling the truth."

"Well, I think that's the first step, then, right? You need to reassure yourself whether or not you're even on the right path before you spend any more time on this."

"I do. But, I also ... Bonnie, I don't want to let you down either."

"Jacob." She put down her scissors and fabric and crossed to stand by him, gently moving his hand till he set down the hammer he had been wielding. Standing in front of him, looking frankly into his face, she scolded him gently. "You know better than that. How many times do I have to tell you?" She smiled. "I support whatever you think is necessary in the name of justice. I trust you. Do what you need to do?"

"Thank you. I still want to take you to supper tonight, though," he said with a wink. "Don't think you're getting out of that."

She laughed. "Oh, don't you worry. I already had a word with Mrs. Everill this morning. She's going to make sure to save the best table for us."

"She's good to you."

"I'm good to her," Bonnie teased.

"You're right," Jacob said. "Of course you're right. I'm going to hurry to finish this up so I can go have a chat with Mr. Towers."

"I think that's the perfect place to start," Bonnie said. "And by the time you get done with your project, I'll be done with mine, and you can walk me home on your way to the general store."

Jacob couldn't help but admire the way Bonnie sat straight and focused on her work, no matter what else was going on around her. It wasn't the first time he had been grateful for her, and it certainly wouldn't be the last.

CHAPTER SIX

Bonnie stayed at Everlasting Hope Church for the rest of the afternoon, remaining after Jacob left to continue his investigation into the crime that Benjamin had been accused of. He made promises to see her again, and soon, though he wanted to support whatever time she chose to commit to the church Nativity play. There was only so much time left before the holiday—and before the judge arrived in Tucson. They would both be busy.

Jacob made it to the general store in the midafternoon. He hoped, without really expecting, that it would be less busy than it had been the day before. He already felt like he was stepping on toes. It would be inconsiderate of him to take too much of Mr. or Mrs. Towers's time to inquire about Benjamin when they should be waiting on their paying customers. But, Jacob reminded himself, saving an innocent young man would be worth a temporary inconvenience. The Towerses wouldn't want Benjamin to be sentenced if he hadn't done anything wrong. Though Jacob didn't think everyone involved would see it that way, he knew what was right.

When he arrived at the store, Jacob couldn't even enter immediately, it was that busy. He found himself holding the door open for a series of women to enter or exit, each thanking him but going on about their business. A small gap in the procession allowed Jacob to dart inside where he immediately made for the sales counter in the back of the store.

Mr. Towers was helping an older woman with a bolt of fabric, Mrs. Towers was helping a younger woman with a selection of glass bowls and a third person stood behind the counter a few rungs up the ladder, stacking boxes of ammunition in a display.

The Towers family had evidently wasted no time in replacing Benjamin. They must have really needed the help this time of year to keep up with the sales. An extra pair of hands could always find work in a general store.

Standing at over six feet tall, Jacob dwarfed most of the people crowding the shop. He was able to catch Mr. Towers's eye over the head of the woman he was helping.

"Is there something I can do for you, Mr. Payne?"

"I need to have a word about Benjamin Wilbourne when you have a moment, sir."

A frown passed across the other man's face but only briefly. Jacob couldn't guess what the shopkeeper might be feeling. He nodded and returned his attention to his customer.

While he waited, Jacob had an opportunity to look around the store, observing how the customers interacted with the Towers and if anything seemed to be different now that Benjamin wasn't there any longer. It may have just been Jacob's assumptions, but it certainly seemed as though the store was more chaotic than usual. It was crowded, yes, but it also seemed as though more customers had questions, that more product needed to be stocked.

"Mr. Payne?"

Jacob turned back toward the sound of his name. Mr. Towers gestured to him to follow him behind the counter, into the back storeroom. The bounty hunter squeezed in between a man looking at hunting knives and a woman chatting to her friend, and followed the storekeeper.

The backroom was dimly lit, with no windows, but bright enough for Jacob to see that it was even more chaotic back here than it had been out front. Entire full barrels were tipped over on to one side, stacks of boxes leaned haphazardly and other boxes were open and partially unpacked, as though someone had left in the middle of a task.

"Sorry about the mess," Mr. Towers said, gesturing vaguely to the room. "We've been ... a bit shorthanded lately. As you know."

"Yes, sir. That's what I wanted to talk to you about. I visited Benjamin at the jail this morning."

"You did?"

Again, Jacob couldn't read his expression.

"Yes, sir. He told me that he was here all day during when the crime was supposed to have taken place. Can you verify that?"

Mr. Towers let out a long sigh. "You know I already talked to the marshal about this, don't you? Didn't he tell you what we said?"

"Some. Not all. I'm trying to go deeper in the investigation than the marshal went. I'm concerned that not all of the information has come to light."

"Well ..." Mr. Towers strode away from Jacob through the uneven stacks of boxes and barrels that filled the room. "The day the marshal asked me about—two days ago, right?—Benjamin had been tasked with setting up a display of weapons and ammunition behind the sales counter, but it all had to be sorted first. The shipments we get from back east are just a mess most of the time. That means he was back here by himself most of the day. We came back periodically to find specific things for customers, but he was alone for hours at a time while he sorted through the various gauges and whatnot."

"I see."

"I wish I could tell you more, Mr. Payne. I don't like to believe that Benjamin could do a thing like this. We've raised him since he was an infant and I had thought he was growing into a fine young man. But ..."

He spread his hands, palms up, helplessly.

"I see," Jacob said. "Thank you, Mr. Towers. And if you think of anything else, I'd appreciate it if you let me know."

"You or the marshal? Isn't he the one in charge of this?"

Jacob paused, not wanting to overstep his bounds, but uncertain of what would happen otherwise. "Both, if possible. Or just me, and I'll make sure he finds out."

"That's fine, Mr. Payne." He nodded. "Now, if you'll excuse me—"

"Of course. I appreciate your time. I'll be hanging around a bit longer waiting for Marshal Santos, as a matter of fact."

Mr. Towers nodded again curtly and exited the storeroom back out to where the customers were thronging around the sales counter. Jacob followed shortly after and quickly decided it would be better for everyone if he waited for the marshal outside of the store. No sooner had Jacob stepped out into the cold sunny afternoon than he saw the thin frame of Marshal Santos striding toward him.

"Thought I'd find you here, Payne. I don't know what you're trying to prove by going to all this trouble. The kid is already in custody. The case is as final as it's going to be."

"Then why are you here?"

The marshal glared at him. "I'm going to let that impertinence pass, Payne. You don't have the faintest idea what you're dealing with."

"I want to believe you."

The marshal grunted. "I'm going to go get one of the family to take us to their home where we can search Benjamin's quarters."

Jacob could imagine the conversation going on inside, as the marshal tried to talk one of the Towers family into leaving their post on such a busy day. He didn't envy the lawman one bit. Every time Jacob thought about settling down and taking a job with less travel and more responsibility, he remembered occasions like this where no matter what the marshal did it would irritate someone.

The bounty hunter laughed to himself, grateful for the fiftieth time that day that he ruled himself, his own life, and that he had found a woman that supported that.

The marshal finally exited the general store, leading their guide. Jacob was shocked to realize that it was the same young lady he had seen stacking ammunition behind the sales counter only a few minutes ago. She must have taken over the job Benjamin had started.

"Payne, you know Elizabeth Towers?" the marshal said. "Miss Towers, this here is Jacob Payne. He's a bounty hunter, but he'll be assisting me today if that's acceptable to you."

The girl nodded meekly. She seemed to be about the same age as Benjamin. Maybe fifteen or sixteen. Jacob hadn't realized that the Towerses had a daughter, let alone one that likely knew their prisoner fairly well.

"Come with me," she said, as she led the two men away from the store.

The Towers family lived only a couple city blocks away from their general store. As they traveled, Elizabeth explained to the two lawmen how her family used to live in the storeroom for the first year after they arrived in the territory.

"And Benjamin stayed there too?" the marshal clarified.

"Oh, no. No, Pa had him stay in a tent on the site of where the house is now. Pa was too afraid that someone might come steal our tools or lumber while we slept, so Benjamin stayed to guard it."

"He was, what? Ten years old then?" Jacob inquired.

Elizabeth nodded. "I think so. About that. He and Pa would do the construction work during the day while Ma and I put the store together."

"And has Benjamin ever seemed unhappy to you, especially recently? Any reason to suspect he might be trying to get out of town or save up money to make it on his own?"

The girl remained looking forward when she answered, leading them to the house. "Um, no. No, I don't— I don't think so."

Just as with the question of Benjamin's guilt,

Jacob felt a sense, an intuition, that there was something else there. Miss Towers knew more than she was saying, but he wasn't going to press it. Not yet at least.

They arrived at the family home in that moment. It was a small, one-story cozy home, with a wide front porch that ran almost the full length of the building. Warm and welcoming, even when empty, Jacob thought he himself might like a home like this one day.

"We'll just take a cursory look around the house, if that's all right with you, Miss Towers. But we do need to see where Benjamin sleeps."

"Of course. Whatever you need to do. Please let me know when you're ready to see his bunk. It's out back, in the shed."

The marshal murmured some instructions to Jacob. "We're looking for the cash still, Payne. It hasn't been recovered and the most likely possibility is that Benjamin hid it away somewhere and was arrested before he could spend it."

"Yes, sir."

"You look here," he gestured around the sitting area, "and I'll look in the kitchen."

Jacob got right to work. There weren't many places to hide several hundred dollars in cash in this room, but he would be thorough. He wanted to eliminate all suspicion that Benjamin could have taken the money.

Jacob carefully removed the half-dozen books that were lined up on the mantel, rifling through the pages looking for loose bills, before replacing them. He checked under all the furniture cushions. He ran his hand along the top of the curtain rod, just in case Benjamin had somehow managed to squirrel away something there.

Jacob even looked through the small woodpile that stood to one side of the fireplace.

There was nothing. No cash or anything else hidden in this family's home.

And he could tell from the marshal's expression that he hadn't found anything either.

"Well," Santos said. "I didn't really expect anything. Seems foolish to put that much money where someone else could find it. Miss Towers, can you show us to where Benjamin sleeps—or I suppose, used to sleep?"

"Come with me," she said timidly.

There was a back door through the kitchen of the home, that took the two men out into the small yard with several outbuildings. Near the farthest corner of the lot was a narrow, windowless shed. From the outside, it looked to be barely big enough for a bed, let alone anything else that a growing boy might need or want.

"Doesn't seem like it should take us long to look through this," the marshal muttered to Jacob.

"You can go ahead and go in," Miss Towers told them when they reached the door. "It's not locked or nothing. I'm going to go back inside. Where it's warmer."

"Thank you, miss," Santos said. "We'll let you know if we find anything."

He opened the door as wide as it would go —which was only about halfway.

The marshal swore under his breath. "No wonder she didn't want to stay here."

Without any sunlight to warm the space, the interior of Benjamin's shed was as cold and dark as a cave. Especially now that they were well into December.

"No wonder he's happy to work a lot," Jacob said. "It must be terrible sleeping in here."

"Yes, well ..." Santos seemed disinclined to discuss the physical comfort of a suspected thief. "Let's make this quick. You take the right; I'll take the left."

And quick it was. Other than a bed and a washstand, Benjamin had very few other belongings at all, let alone anywhere that could hide that much in cash. In short order, the two men had touched every single thing in the shed, including overturning the cot on which Benjamin slept and rifling through the pockets of the few pieces of clothing they had found.

"There's nothing here," Jacob said, finally. "There's no cash anywhere here. He didn't do this, Marshal."

Santos looked at Jacob, not glaring, not agreeing, but simply resigned to the truth.

CHAPTER SEVEN

Jacob Payne walked with Marshal Owen Santos away from the Towers home, each quiet and contemplative in his own thoughts. From Jacob's point of view, this seemed to be yet another point in his favor—how could anyone believe Benjamin had stolen that money, especially as said money was nowhere to be found in his belongings.

But this was not a definitive enough piece of evidence to let the kid out of his jail cell, especially in light of everything else.

"Marshal," he began.

"Don't start with me, Payne. You know full well that not finding the money is no proof of anything."

"No, you're right. You're right. I wasn't

going to argue that. It's circumstantial, but I know it's not enough. No, I was going to ask you who the eyewitness was that claims to have seen him leaving the telegraph office."

They had reached the main street of Tucson then, passed by noisy coaches and laughing children chasing each other in a game of tag. All around Jacob was evidence of joy and freedom. All while Benjamin Wilbourne sat in prison for a crime that the bounty hunter could not believe he had done.

Marshal Santos turned to face Jacob, his hands on his hips. He was one of the few men that was taller than Jacob Payne, and was currently using that to his advantage.

"I'll tell you, Payne, but I need you to promise me something."

"Anything."

Santos frowned. "I don't like this. I don't like that you're questioning my authority, but even more than that, I don't like that we might have an innocent man locked up. I'm going to tell you about the eyewitness, but I need your word that if—or when—you discover information that could exonerate Wilbourne that you come straight to me. I want to make this right if there's any right to be had."

"Of course, Marshal. I wouldn't think of doing anything else."

"And you know that if we are able to prove he didn't do this, that might not be enough if we're not able to discover who did do it."

"I was thinking the same thing."

"Do your best. I trust you. I can't do anything more than I am doing, but whatever you find I'll consider."

"I understand, Marshal."

Five minutes later, Jacob was on his way to the musical instrument store that sat next to the telegraph office that Benjamin was alleged to have robbed. Though the marshal got an eyewitness statement from the store proprietor there just the day before, Jacob needed to double check. He had some questions.

Entering the store from the cold outside, Jacob was surprised to find that it wasn't nearly as crowded as the general store or the cafe had been. Evidently Tucson citizens didn't need huge expensive pianos at the end of December. Jacob was grateful for this turn of events—it meant that he would have more time to interrogate the witness, and potentially also meant that she would have had more time and space to accurately see what happened next door.

"Yes?"

An older, stern voice greeted Jacob as he stood near the doorway to the store. He hurried to remove his hat, while turning to see a tall, ramrod-straight woman with stark white hair entering the room. She was dressed in the drabbest, plainest black gown he had ever seen, even more so than some of the mourning the women in his family had worn.

The owner of this store was very clearly a no-nonsense kind of woman; Jacob knew he would have to stick to facts to stay on her good side.

"Yes, ma'am. Thank you, ma'am. I'm here on behalf of Marshal Santos and I have some questions for you about what you saw yesterday. It's Mrs. Hyke, isn't it?"

She frowned, and clasped her hands in front of her, standing even more straight, though Jacob didn't see how that could be possible.

"I told the marshal everything I have to say," she said dismissively. "And if you're not here to buy a piano or stringed instrument or anything at all, you're just wasting my time."

Jacob looked around at the small, cramped room. He couldn't even imagine the cost she must have incurred to ship all of these instruments out from the east coast. It seemed absurd to simply pay for a piano to be sitting here waiting for a buyer, instead of ordering one from a shop when it was called for. But—he looked back at Mrs. Hyke—he also couldn't rightly suspect she was a woman who didn't know what she was doing.

In a quick moment, Jacob decided there was a reason he would never be a businessman. He elected to not question a single thing that she did for her store.

Immediately after that thought, he resolved to purchase something from her. Maybe it would warm her to him, and make her more inclined to answer his questions.

"I understand, ma'am," he said. "We just had some follow-up questions for you. The circuit judge will be here very soon, you see, and we wanted to make sure the case against the accused is solid. I had been planning to purchase a ... um ..."

Jacob looked around at the shop for inspiration. He had nowhere to keep a piano, and no idea how to play any of the other instruments he could see. He turned back toward Mrs. Hyke and his eyes lit on a small pyramid of yellow boxes on the counter next to her.

"Harmonica," he concluded. "I was planning on buying myself a harmonica to take with me when I go out on the road after outlaws and I told the marshal I'd be happy to ask you some questions since I was going to be coming here anyway."

Mrs. Hyke softened slightly at his pronouncement, but Jacob still knew to be cautious. She was like an injured cat; the slightest wrong move and she would turn tail or hiss.

"A harmonica?" she asked, dubiously.

"That's right. I've been missing having music in my life since I came out west—my late wife used to play the piano, you see. A harmonica is a small thing I can take with me."

"Very well. I only have one model, but I suppose that will be sufficient for you?"

"I'm sure it will be," he averred, stepping up to the counter and the display of instruments. "And, like I mentioned, I wonder if I could ask you some questions about what you saw the other day?"

Jacob pulled out his billfold as he said that; he was careful to hold it at such an angle that Mrs. Hyke could see that he had plenty of cash on hand to back-up his claim of buying a harmonica. He couldn't risk having this backfire now.

She met his eye, then nodded brusquely. "Very well. As I told the marshal, I was here in my shop on the afternoon in question, and I saw the suspected thief walking quickly away from the scene of the crime. His hands were in his coat pockets, and there seemed to be some kind of bulge, as though he was carrying something. I assumed that was the money he had stolen, though I didn't see anything myself."

"I see." Jacob looked through the front window of the shop. There was only one, though it was large. "And were you standing right about here?"

"At first, but there was no one else in the store at that time, so I hurried over to the window."

From this angle, there was very little of the street that Mrs. Hyke could have seen. Although, if she happened to be looking at precisely the right moment, there was a clear view to the street outside.

"And, Mrs. Hyke, can you describe the person you saw?"

"Of course," she bristled. "He was tall and thin, though perhaps not so tall as you. Dark hair, dark clothes, though not so dark that I couldn't see he was about covered in dust. Evidently hygiene was not one of his priorities."

"Can you tell me anything else about him? Age? Was he smoking? His skin?"

Mrs. Hyke frowned. "Well, there was only a moment, but I would say he is younger than you though not a child. I'm sorry, at my age it seems impossible to guess anyone's age anymore."

"I understand. Any other detail you can remember?"

"Well ... no, I'm sorry. You mentioned his skin, but all I can recall is that he seemed dirty all over, his clothes and his hair. But ... You understand it was so fast."

"I understand. And ... I'm sorry, Mrs. Hyke, but did you tell the marshal this yesterday? That he was maybe a bit younger than me and the most defining characteristic of his skin was that he seemed dirty? No scars or ... other things?"

Jacob was trying very hard not to lead Mrs. Hyke to say anything in particular, but it seemed utterly impossible to believe that she could have seen one of the only Black citizens of town and not comment on it.

"I thought I had. He didn't ask specifically the same questions, though, so perhaps I told him other details. The man's gun or something similar."

"A gun," he repeated. "You're positive about that. You saw his gun. Could you describe it?"

"Oh, heaven's no." She waved at him dismissively. "I haven't any use for a gun. I just know that I could see his holster on his hip, with the butt of some kind of weapon poking up out of it."

Jacob nodded. "Thank you, Mrs. Hyke. This has been very helpful. We're very grateful to you."

"Will you need me to testify?"

"I'm not sure. We'll do our best to make this as smooth as possible for you. But the marshal or myself might come back to discuss that further."

"Very well." She was nothing if not matter-of-fact. "I aim to be an upstanding citizen of this territory I've chosen as my home. If I am needed, I accept that."

"Thank you."

"But, please, Mr. Payne, don't be interrupting my work and my customers any more than necessary."

He stifled a grin, handing over the necessary cash to purchase the musical instrument he had promised.

"I won't, ma'am."

CHAPTER EIGHT

Jacob Payne left Mrs. Hyke's store with his mind whirring. Through all of his investigation, he kept discovering more and more clues that Benjamin Wilbourne was innocent of the charge of theft for which he was currently sitting in a jail cell. In spite of all of this, Jacob knew that it wasn't yet enough to free him.

Adding doubt to the conviction was one thing, but doubt was not evidence of innocence.

Jacob would need something more definitive —something like discovering the actual perpetrator. Finding the cash would be even better.

But he had no idea how to do that.

All he had was a rough description from Mrs. Hyke, and the same small circumstantial clues that also pointed to Benjamin Wilbourne.

Who in town had come into a lot of money in the last day or two? Who in town had been (or had a reputation for being) dirty and unhygienic? Who would smoke or not notice if they dropped a button?

There were too many questions to answer.

And on top of that Jacob now owned a harmonica.

Jacob laughed to himself, as he walked through the cold winter street of Tucson. He hadn't learned anything new worth taking back to the marshal. No, what he needed right now was a hot meal and some time to think over all he had learned and what his next step would be.

Turning left at the next corner, Jacob made his way to the San Xavier Cafe. He had plans to meet Bonnie there, one of the few times they would be eating together instead of her waiting on him as he ate.

He wondered if she would want to continue to work if he were to propose.

The thought almost stopped him in his tracks. He stumbled briefly, recovering his balance as he thought over this realization.

Jacob didn't want to be grabbing dinner at the cafe, even if his sweetheart was waiting for him there. Jacob wanted to be heading to his own home, his own warm fire, where he could share a meal with his wife. Or, maybe he could even wait on her. Lord knew the woman deserved to be treated the best he could offer.

That settled it. Maybe it was the cold night; maybe it was the thought of being innocently accused; maybe it was simply that enough time had passed and he was ready. But there in the middle of the Tucson street, just at sunset, Jacob Payne decided the time had come and he would propose to Bonnie Loft.

He would not stall any longer.

He could not risk losing her.

Jacob arrived at the cafe, threw open the door and immediately locked eyes with his love. Though every bone in his body screamed at him to take her in his arms, he knew he didn't want to embarrass her in public with any display of emotion she might not be ready for.

Instead, he waved, smiled, and began to cross the room to her to share their meal.

No sooner had he taken a few steps into the cafe, than Jacob felt a hand on his shoulder. As he was turning to see who wanted his attention, Pastor Ambrose stood next to him.

"Mr. Payne! I'm delighted to find you here. Miss Loft suggested I might, and as usual she was right. Come over to the bar."

He sat heavily on a stool while Jacob

remained standing. He was puzzled. He looked over his shoulder to where Bonnie was giving him a quizzical look.

"What can I get for you boys?" Mickey asked, appearing behind the bar.

"I'm meeting Bonnie," Jacob said, pointing over his shoulder and hoping the pastor would take a hint.

"Oh, I've already eaten," the pastor said. "I just need a word with Mr. Payne and then I'll free up my seat."

"See that you do," Mickey said sullenly, before moving to help the next man over.

"Can I help you with something, sir?" Jacob asked Pastor Ambrose.

"You can." Pastor Ambrose turned so his body was completely facing Jacob. "You can. I need you, Mr. Payne. I don't think there's anyone else I can turn to."

Jacob heard the desperation in the man's voice; past the flattery, it was clear he really was hoping for the bounty hunter's help.

"Is there something wrong with the manger I built?"

As he asked that, he felt another, smaller, hand rest on his other side. Jacob turned to see Bonnie Loft standing with her face lit up in expectation.

"Bonnie! I'm sorry. The pastor here waylaid me on my—"

"No, no, don't worry," she assured him. "I just wanted to see if there was anything I can do. I'm sorry. I was the one who told Pastor Ambrose he would find you here."

Her gentle smile made him feel to bursting with admiration. For a brief moment, Jacob felt self-conscious that he had only just moments before decided to propose to this wonderful woman, but now in the bright light and crowd of the cafe it seemed too crass, too bold.

"I'm glad he found you," she continued.

Jacob blinked in surprise and looked back and forth between his two friends. "What's wrong?"

"Oh, nothing, nothing," the pastor assured him. "That is, nothing that's not fixable. It's just that ... well, we seem to be short a person for our Nativity play tomorrow. I know you're generally a busy man, but Bonnie assured me that you would love to do it."

"I'm sorry ... I ..." Jacob stuttered. He glanced at Bonnie who nodded at him encouragingly. "You need me to what? I don't understand."

"We need a Joseph," Bonnie blurted out.

"A Joseph?" Jacob repeated.

"Joseph," Pastor Ambrose said. "For the Nativity play. Marshal Santos had promised to do it but he now tells us that the circuit judge will be in town right when we plan to be holding the performance. We need another tall man, someone with presence and honor, to play the role of Saint Joseph, husband of Mary, in the Nativity play. You were our first choice."

"Me? Joseph?"

"And you're not planning on leaving town again, right, Jacob?" Bonnie asked hesitantly. "I know that's what you had told me, but I also know that you might need to change your mind."

Jacob's mind spun at all the commitments he had tied himself to and all he still needed to accomplish in order to free Benjamin Wilbourne. But, then, how could he say no to Bonnie?

"I would so love if you were able to help with this," she said. "I'll be there the whole time, helping with the costumes."

"Costumes?"

All three of them turned to the fourth voice, the man who was inserting himself into their conversation. It was Clifford Pierce, talkative as ever.

"You're not thinking of putting this man in a

costume, are you, Pastor?" Pierce laughed and clapped a hand to Jacob's shoulder.

He felt surrounded, pressure from all sides.

"Why, yes, Mr. Pierce," the pastor said. "I think he'd make a wonderful Joseph."

"As you say. But if you'd like, I'm happy to set aside my shepherd's robes to step up. Only if you need me to, that is. I just want to serve the Lord where I'm needed most."

"You are going to be in the Nativity play?" Jacob asked, shocked.

"I certainly am," Pierce responded with faux indignation. "Coleman and me and a couple other fellas agreed to help out. It's all for the glory of God, ain't it? I'm not one to be too proud to take on a little ol' task for the church."

At this pronouncement, Jacob happened to catch a glimpse of Bonnie's face—she was proud and admiring, listening to this other man's willingness to help. Jacob knew he couldn't let her down. Though he still didn't know how he was going to be able to prove that Benjamin Wilbourne had not robbed that telegraph office, Jacob reasoned that by the time the Nativity began, the judge would already be here. He would have to solve this problem before he needed to get in the costume either way.

"All right," he said, to Bonnie first, before

turning to the pastor. "I'll help you. Just tell me what to do."

Bonnie threw her arms around his neck. "Thank you! Thank you. This will be so wonderful. Thank you."

Jacob caught Mickey's grin as he delivered a plate to the man sitting next to Jacob, suspicious that the bartender had been eavesdropping on the whole thing. As Jacob tried to imagine himself in the biblical robes that would make up his costume, he groaned to himself, wondering how many of his friends would show up in church just to see him like that.

But, he thought to himself, maybe Pierce is right. It's for a good cause, after all.

CHAPTER NINE

The following morning, Jacob woke up early and abruptly. Like a bolt of lightning, he remembered that the fifteen-year-old Benjamin Wilbourne still sat in the Tucson jail, accused of a crime that Jacob was certain he had not committed, though he was as yet unable to prove it.

Jacob had talked to everyone involved, so far as he knew. There was Mr. Wood left to speak to, the shop owner who was robbed. Though he didn't see anything directly, Jacob didn't know how much help he could be. Jacob sighed and realized he had to try. He had to go over and talk to the victim.

And then after he made that final interview,

Jacob would go see the marshal again, reporting back. Whether he learned anything new or not.

He could figure this out. Jacob was sure that he could find the evidence needed to free the young man—he just wasn't positive he would have time to do it before the circuit judge showed up.

The bounty hunter was out the door only a few minutes later. It was still early enough in the morning that he wondered if he would beat the shop owner there, but he was relieved to find that such concern was unfounded.

Jacob approached the storefront confidently, stepping up just as Mr. Wood was unlocking his front door.

"Mr. Payne?" the man said. He was a portly man, both tall and wide, taking up much of the space in front of the door. "I don't believe we've met, but the marshal and his deputies have told me enough about you that I'm sure I'm not mistaken."

"No, you're not." Jacob smiled and shook the man's hand. "I'm honored that my fame precedes me."

Wood laughed. "Oh, well, I think it's more that the deputies are just trying to make me feel safer. They've assured me at least a half a dozen times that if anything ever happened here, that you'd be on the case. And look! They were right. Here you are. Though, I had assumed they meant before the case was solved."

At that, Mr. Wood opened the door and let the two of them into the dark shop. Jacob hovered near the front door, respectfully, waiting for his host to light a lamp and conduct what he needed to do to begin work for the day.

"I was thinking I'd make some coffee, Mr. Payne. Can I tempt you?" He bent over to light a fire in the small stove in the corner of the shop.

"I'd appreciate that, yes, sir."

"I assume you're here to talk about the robbery the other day? The marshal told me I might need to testify."

"Yes, I ..." Jacob cleared his throat, unsure where to start. "The judge will be here tonight, though I'm not sure what testimony you will need. The marshal filled me in on what evidence was found, but I thought I'd check to see if anything else had come to mind since you gave your statement. Any other details you've discovered or remembered?"

"Oh, now, let me think," he said as he checked the kettle for water. "Well, as you likely know, I had closed up for supper that day. I could have sworn I locked up behind me, but seeing as the place wasn't broken into it's possible I was mistaken. I'm always so careful, though."

"I understand," Jacob said. "It's hard when we can blame ourselves."

"Precisely." Mr. Wood took a deep breath before continuing. "So, when I returned from the cafe, I was dismayed to find that the door of the shop was unlocked. It was closed, so I was afforded a small moment of believing that no harm had come from my forgetting to lock it. I entered and ..." He spread his hands wide and shrugged, self-deprecatingly. "I was wrong."

"Yes ..." Jacob hesitated. "I'm sorry that we haven't recovered that cash yet."

He shook his head. It smelled like the coffee was close to being done. Jacob wanted to gently guide him to talking about the other clues he had come across, but didn't want to rush him.

"I'm not bitter," Mr. Wood replied as he pulled two tin coffee mugs out of a cupboard behind his counter. "I knew I was at risk at any time—which, incidentally, is why I always tried to keep my door locked. But ..." He shook his head again. "I won't deny that it is mighty frustrating."

The large man poured two steaming hot cups of coffee and Jacob took a deep breath, smelling the roasted beans and being grateful for generous neighbors. He accepted the cup of coffee and took a drink, reveling in the taste and smell before continuing.

"The marshal told me you had found some sign of the intruder when you got back?" he prompted.

"Oh! Yes. I did. I walked in and immediately smelled that someone had smoked in here. There's no smoking allowed in my shop," he said sternly to Jacob, as though he were getting ready to roll a cigarette. "I'm very cautious of fire. I don't allow any of my customers to do it, and I'm sure no one who had come in that morning had even tried. After careful searching, I found a cigarette butt back here behind the counter."

"Is there anything you recognized about it?"

"No." He shook his head. "I've never been a smoker. I couldn't tell you the difference between one kind of tobacco or another. But I did know enough to leave it where it was, until the marshal came to inspect everything."

"That was good thinking," Jacob said.

"I found it back behind the counter where I keep the cash box. Actually." He held up one finger as though to pause the conversation. "Where I *used to* keep the cash box. I take it

home with me every night now, and I've
ordered a large safe to be sent out from the
east." He shook his head again. "I was so reck-
less. This is all my own fault."

"That might be a little extreme," Jacob said,
hesitatingly. "After all ... the thief did knowingly
break the law. His choices are not your fault."

"Even so," Mr. Wood said. "I will be more
cautious from now on."

Jacob nodded, drinking more of his coffee.
"Did you notice anything besides the cigarette?"

"I did, yes. A button. It had fallen not far
from the counter somewhere ..." He gestured to
the middle of the room near where Jacob was
standing. "Somewhere over there. I am always
sure to keep the floor as spotless as possible. It
makes the customers feel more comfortable,
you see. I am absolutely certain the button was
not there when I left for my mid-day meal."

"Is there anything remarkable about that
button?"

At this point, Jacob felt like he was grasping.
Nothing Mr. Wood had told him would in any
way exonerate Benjamin Wilbourne.

He shrugged. "Not particularly. I didn't look
carefully, but it seemed like the kind of button
that could be on any kind of piece of clothing."

"Did you ...?" Jacob searched his brain for

the little he knew about clothing. "Were there any threads or fabric attached to it or ... I'm sorry. I don't know what to ask here. I'm not sure what the judge will need in order to convict the thief."

"You're not alone, friend. I was afraid to touch anything once I discovered the money was missing. I didn't know what the marshal would need or not need to see."

Jacob rubbed his temple.

All of this felt circular. The evidence all pointed to Benjamin just enough that no one looked any further. But even when he tried to look further, Jacob was still only finding the same evidence that the marshal had found.

There must be something more. There must be something that someone wasn't saying or a direction he wasn't yet looking.

"Well," he said, finally, "thank you for all your help, Mr. Wood. If you think of anything else, I would appreciate it if you sent word to the marshal or me."

"Of course. And if you have more questions I'm happy to answer. Anything that will help recover the cash that boy stole is my top priority."

"Yes ... well ..." Jacob hesitated, unsure if he was overstepping. "To tell you the truth, Mr.

Wood, I don't have much hope of that. We searched his quarters and didn't find even a single note. If Benjamin had the cash, he's hidden it well."

Wood's face clouded; this was undoubtedly not what he had been hoping to hear.

He took a deep breath.

"Well, again, Mr. Payne, please let me know what I can do to help the investigation."

"Thank you. We'll be in touch."

Jacob offered the coffee mug back to the shopkeeper, tipped his hat and exited the store. Standing out on the boardwalk, he looked around helplessly. Dead end after dead end. Maybe he would just have to reconcile himself to Benjamin's getting the rope.

CHAPTER TEN

Jacob still had a few hours before he needed to report to the Everlasting Hope Church for his turn as Joseph in the Nativity play. He had been hoping that all of this additional investigating he was doing would have some kind of result. He had been hoping that he could spend this time going over the new revelations with the marshal, convincing him of Benjamin's innocence, getting him out of that jail cell and maybe even inviting the kid to come to church with him.

But as the bounty hunter strode down the streets of Tucson without goal or purpose, he realized he had never been more disappointed in himself. Time was up and he had failed.

When a wagon drawn by two charcoal-black

horses rolled by, Jacob was reminded of someone who might still need him: his horse Blaze. With renewed energy, he turned the next corner to make his way to the livery where Caleb Shaw always took such good care of Jacob's mount in the weeks that he was in Tucson.

When he entered the stable, Caleb was busy brushing down another horse, but nodded when he saw Jacob. Not many men came to just visit their horses, but Jacob had never been like other men. As he stepped into the stall, Blaze must have recognized his scent and visibly perked up.

"Hey there, fella," Jacob said softly, reaching up to scratch between the horse's ears. "You having a good break? You makin' some friends in here?"

Blaze nuzzled Jacob's coat, looking for the carrots or other treats that he always brought.

"You're right. You found them. You got me." Jacob laughed as he offered the vegetables to his horse.

While Blaze munched on the carrots, Jacob thought about all the pieces that were missing in the case he was trying to solve. Someone knew something; he just had to figure out who that was.

After a few silent minutes, Jacob heard boot steps on the ground coming toward him.

"What are you doing here, Payne?" Clifford Pierce said as he approached.

He walked up to the horse and rider slowly, letting Blaze get his scent and grow accustomed to a new person. Jacob was grateful. Though Pierce tended to irritate him in other ways, there was no doubt that he was a good horseman and a good bounty hunter. Not quite as good as Jacob himself, but certainly deserving of respect.

"What are you doing here?" Jacob countered. "I didn't think I'd be seeing you till the church later today."

"Oh, I forgot I left a box of bullets in my saddle bag, and I came to claim it." He held up the box he must have only retrieved. "I'm supposed to meet Coleman for a drink before we head over to the church."

"That's right. I had forgotten he was going to be part of the play as well. Tell me again, Pierce. How did you meet that fella?"

He shrugged. "Cards. Whiskey. You know. Same way we meet pretty much anyone new to town."

"That's what I figured."

"Why do you ask?"

"Oh ... I just ..." Jacob continued to stroke Blaze's neck while he thought about the best way to word it. "I'm not sure. He just strikes me as the kind of man to pay attention to."

"Gut feeling, is it?" Clifford suggested, nodding sagely. "I had the same feeling. In fact, the first few days he was in town I stuck really close to him. Made sure to find out where he's staying and try to get him to take every meal with me."

"Did that work?"

He shrugged. "Some. Hit and miss. I certainly spent a lot of time with the man. That feeling never went away, though."

"Hm," Jacob mused. "Thank you, Pierce. Glad to know my feeling's not mistaken."

"I don't think he truly caught on to what I was doing, though," Pierce said with a laugh. "Poor man musta thought I was real lonely. Once, a couple days ago, he even suggested someone else I should invite to eat with instead of himself. So I wouldn't be lonely, I'd wager. Mr. Wood looked mighty shocked to get the invite, tell you the truth. Not sure he leaves his shop all that often."

Jacob frowned and turned all his focus on Pierce. Blaze began to nuzzle Jacob's neck and ear, pleading for more attention. "Mr. Wood? Is that what you said?"

"Sure was. Closed his store up and everything for a dinner break. He and I went over to the San Xavier. Your girl wasn't working then, though. He's a nice man. I hadn't previously had the pleasure of too much conversation, but did you know that he came out to the territory when he was only ten? His parents were missionaries and—"

Jacob held up a hand to forestall another of Pierce's longwinded stories. "Hang on, I just need to— Wood, you said. Wood closed up his telegraph office to have dinner with you because your friend Coleman suggested it?"

Pierce paused, and rubbed his chin through his beard, as though thinking carefully. "Yes, I suppose that's all correct. Why do you ask?"

"I was just talking to him..." Jacob trailed off, his mind whirring over all the possibilities and what this could mean. Wood hadn't mentioned leaving to see Pierce, but maybe that was just a harmless oversight. Was Pierce in any way part of this? Jacob scrutinized the other man—his friend —taking in his blank expression and everything that he knew about the other bounty hunter.

This new piece of information was both

potentially   helpful   and   maddeningly
incomplete.

What did it mean?

"Do you know where Coleman is now?"

The look Pierce gave him was part amuse-
ment, part condescension.

"Payne, I have no ever-loving idea where he
is this second. I'm not his keeper."

"You're right. I'm sorry, I just—"

"But I know where he will be," Pierce
added. "So do you. I just told you I'm meeting
him for a drink, and then later he's supposed to
be one of the shepherds at church later.
Remember? You'll be there, won't you? You're
not gonna make me make excuses for you to
your girl."

"I'll be there." He glanced quickly at his
pocket watch. "I just have a lot to do before
then."

Pierce chuckled. "You always got something.
You really should try to relax more, Payne
Enjoy life."

"I will. After this last thing."

Pierce was still laughing when Payne told his
horse good-bye and darted out of the livery
again.

CHAPTER ELEVEN

When he had been a little boy, Jacob Payne's father used to let him help with some of the plantation chores for a small wage. Looking back now, Jacob realized that his family owned all the slaves they needed to get the job done, but his father had taken Jacob's energy and ambition and directed it such that he could learn a life lesson as well.

The family had a small orchard, mostly just for the family and everyone living on the plantation, but still large enough to be a project. When he turned ten years old, Jacob's father offered to pay him one cent for every five bushels of apples he picked. It wasn't much. It could take him all day to pick enough to make thirty cents. His hands were small; he could only grab one apple at a time and was slower in carrying them all back to the shed where they were stored, sorted and loaded up for the local market. But Jacob reveled in the physical labor and in the pride of knowing that he had been the one to clear that tree or row of trees.

The following year, when the apple harvest came around, Jacob asked his father if he could pick all of the apples—every single one of them. Their orchard wasn't over-large—it was one of several different crops that their plantation grew—but even so it was a daunting task.

Jacob's father had laughed at him, had assumed at first that the boy was kidding. Such a job would be all but impossible for a boy of his age.

But Jacob had insisted. He had pleaded. He was determined.

Jacob had seen the prettiest delicate gold chain necklace the last time he had gone to town with his mother and wanted so badly to buy it for her for Christmas. He had a goal, and he had means to achieve the goal, albeit on a path that was full of obstacles and hardships. Still, he was sure he could do it.

After several days of pleading, Jacob finally wore his father down. The boy was warned to be careful, and was made to promise that he would come tell his father as soon as he thought he couldn't complete the task. There was a time limit, after all. Jacob knew this. The apples all needed to be off the trees before they began to rot, or before winter hit their part of Virginia.

But Jacob wasn't about to admit defeat.

Throughout the weeks that he had available, Jacob was in the orchard from dawn until dusk six days each week. His hands developed blisters, that popped and healed and blistered again, all the while giving him a thick, hard skin to equip him for further difficult work.

At one point he fell off a ladder and dislocated his shoulder. Even now more than two decades later Jacob could remember the pain of that injury and the subsequent treatment. He had to rest one of his arms, making the job that much more difficult. Jacob even thought about enlisting his brothers to help, promising them part of his earnings, but he dismissed that thought quickly.

He could do this. He was doing this. He was doing it all on his own. It was taking longer, and was more of a sacrifice than he had anticipated, but he wasn't about to quit.

Harvesting the apples from the entire orchard took him right up until the deadline. There was a small flurry of snowflakes during the final afternoon as he lugged bushel after bushel back to the shed. His fingers were growing numb as he clutched the baskets. It was too hard for him to grasp the apples with gloves on, so he had gone without.

That final evening, he stumbled home cold, sore and miserable but exhilarated. He had done it. He had set his goal and gone to every length necessary to accomplish it. His mother had been so surprised and pleased by his gift to her that every blister, sore muscle and pre-dawn wake-up call had been worth it.

Jacob had never forgotten that fall. He didn't ever undertake such a commitment at his family's orchard again, but once was enough. Through this he learned early that he could do anything he set his mind to doing. No matter what the obstacles, if he was persistent and focused, he would succeed.

Since becoming a bounty hunter, there was a time in every case where Jacob began to doubt that he would be able to apprehend the criminal, but that doubt never lasted long. He always had a wealth of tools and resources at his disposal, and he always knew that he could out-work, out-shoot or out-smart his opponent.

This time, however, trying to find the evidence to exonerate a jailed boy, simply based on a hunch he had, Jacob was losing hope. Maybe he had backed the wrong horse.

The sun was climbing in the sky and the streets of Tucson were filling with citizens traveling to visit friends or treat themselves to a meal out or just bask in the winter sun. After trying to politely elbow his way past one too many bodies, Jacob finally gave up and stepped into the dirt alongside the wooden boardwalk. He had to get to the marshal's office as soon as possible.

As he burst through the door of the office, panting slightly from his run, Jacob found the marshal standing behind his desk.

"I think I know who robbed the telegraph office," Jacob blurted out. "I just need more time."

The marshal looked at him and shook his head sadly.

"I'm sorry, Payne," the marshal said. "But Wilbourne has already been transferred to the courthouse."

"What?" the bounty hunter exclaimed. "I thought— I still have several hours. You can't do this. He's innocent!"

"Jacob." The marshal spoke softly, kindly. Using Jacob's first name took the bounty hunter by surprise, but also prompted him to listen more carefully. "It's Christmas Eve. The judge is here now, and we can't very well ask him to delay hearing the case just because you have a hunch."

"But ..." Jacob stammered. "I just need ... I just need a little more time."

Santos shook his head. "I'll see what I can do. If I can get Wilbourne to be the last case on the docket that should give you maybe two hours. Maybe. But, I gotta say, Payne ... I don't know what you think you're going to find in the next couple hours that you haven't already. Especially seeing as you're supposed to be at the Everlasting Hope Church."

Jacob groaned. It was not that he had forgotten he had committed to the nativity play for Bonnie and Pastor Ambrose. It was just that ... he thought he would have more time. How could he possibly find the irrefutable proof before Benjamin's case was heard?

One thing at a time.

Jacob rotated his shoulder, the one that had been dislocated. The injury that had slowed him down on his path toward earning his wage. Slowed, but not stopped.

That's what this was. An obstacle. Not a wall.

He could figure this out. He just had to start. One apple at a time. One clue at a time.

The first thing Jacob had to do was get over to the other side of Tucson. Knowing that Benjamin had already been transferred to the courthouse meant there was nothing else here for him. Except ...

"Marshal, has the evidence in Benjamin's case been transferred?"

"Not yet." Santos gestured to a wooden crate on his desk. "That's what I came back for. All the evidence for his and the other cases is here."

"Can I just have second look at that cigarette and button?" Jacob asked. "I have a thought, but don't want to be accusing the wrong party if I can help it."

He hadn't intended for that last sentence to come out so biting, but he couldn't help himself. Jacob was frustrated. But the marshal complied graciously, handing over two separate unsealed envelopes.

One held a cigarette butt. Jacob opened it, and took a whiff. He recognized the tobacco, but so many men smoked that kind he wasn't sure it would lead anywhere.

The second envelope held the button. Pulling it out—careful not to drop it—Jacob turned it over in his fingers. The first thing that struck him was the fact that this was clearly a worn button. He couldn't even imagine the possibility that this was a new button that Benjamin had stolen from the general store, which was the marshal's current hypothesis.

If anything, this piece of evidence pointed away from Benjamin Wilbourne.

But Jacob didn't have time for that argument with the marshal. He still had to gather more evidence.

"You're off to the courthouse now?"

The marshal nodded.

"Stall. As long as you can."

CHAPTER TWELVE

Jacob Payne ran. He was already late to the Everlasting Hope Church. Promising Bonnie that he would take on the role of Joseph in the Nativity play had been easy when all he wanted was to please her, when he was sure that it would be easy to discover who had robbed the telegraph office and he could free Benjamin Wilbourne.

The one thing he kept holding on to through all of his hurrying was the fact that Coleman would also be at the church. Jacob could keep an eye on him at the very least. The man was a good enough Christian to volunteer to be part of the Nativity play, but that didn't mean that Jacob's gut feeling about him was going to go away.

Jacob burst through the wide front doors of the church and strode down the aisle into the dim light. As his eyes adjusted, he noticed Bonnie on the left side of the altar, sitting and studiously sewing buttons on to a wide swath of fabric that was draped across her lap.

He looked around at the rest of the participants.

Clifford Pierce sat in the front row of the church, dressed in one of the rough cloth robes that Bonnie had been sewing all week. On one side sat Coleman in another robe, with several other men and women gathered around. Pierce was holding court, telling a story that made his listeners laugh and gasp alternately.

Jacob knew it was likely some embellished tale of one of the outlaws the man had captured. He *had* captured them, after all, so Jacob tried not to begrudge him the attention he so loved.

But he wouldn't be joining that group.

Instead, he went straight to where Bonnie sat.

"Still at it?" he asked.

She smiled up at him, but didn't cease in her sewing. "Mrs. Cicero's oldest boy got the flu, so I've been on my own in this. I should have just enough time to finish this last costume before everyone starts arriving, though."

"Can I help with anything?"

"No. Thank you. But you can put your own costume on." She indicated with a nod to a robe draped over a nearby chair. "That one's yours."

"I can do that," he assured her.

With the robe on over his clothes, Jacob couldn't easily check the time. He would just have to bide his time. He almost wished the Nativity play was starting soon so he would have something to distract himself with, rather than think about Benjamin Wilbourne being brought up before a judge.

"That's strange," Bonnie mumbled to herself. "I wonder if Mr. Coleman knows he's missing a button."

Jacob's head whipped around. "What did you say?"

She blinked up at him, confused, as though surprised that she had said something out loud. "Oh, it's nothing. I just noticed that Mr. Coleman's vest here is missing a button and wondered if he realized it. I'd sew on a replacement if I had one handy, but I don't think I have time to run to the general store."

"Can I see?"

She handed him the vest without comment

and moved on to the next costume in her pile. Jacob held the garment close to his face—he wanted to be sure he wasn't mistaken. There were three other buttons still on the vest, all matching and all worn evenly, as one would expect if they rubbed against the inside of a coat regularly. Though Jacob didn't have the original button found at the crime scene, he was positive that it matched the ones he saw here. The color, the shape, and even the way they were worn and used.

This was it. This was the last piece of evidence he needed to poke a hole in what the marshal was presenting as the case against Wilbourne.

"Bonnie," he said quietly. "You're absolutely sure this vest belongs to Andrew Coleman."

"Yes. He took it off and kind of threw it at me when I handed him the costume he's wearing now." She frowned, but didn't complain more.

The disrespect of throwing it at someone was just one more offense piled on top of others. Coleman needed to be in that jail cell where Benjamin had been the last couple days.

The bounty hunter had to get to the courthouse as soon as possible.

As soon as he looked up and began to make

his way to the door, he felt a hand on his arm. Pastor Ambrose was tugging him toward the altar.

"It's your cue, Mr. Payne," the pastor hissed at him. "Go out there and be Joseph."

The vest was pulled from his hands, and his Mary—Mrs. Rogers, the schoolteacher—linked her arm in his. Jacob felt a gentle nudge from behind as he was thrust up the steps of the altar where he would pretend to be present for the birth of Jesus Christ.

While God's son was saving mankind, all Jacob could think about was how he could save one fifteen-year-old boy.

CHAPTER THIRTEEN

The Nativity play seemed to go on forever. Jacob writhed inside at the fact that minutes were ticking by. He had more evidence that might get Benjamin Wilbourne declared not guilty, but it might not be enough. And even if it was enough, it wasn't at the court for his case. It wasn't added into evidence.

Every moment that went by, as Jacob knelt with head bowed by the manger he had built, the bounty hunter prayed over and over that he would somehow have enough time to save the poor kid.

"I proclaim to you good news that brings great joy to all the people..."

One of the young men whose family lived in

Tucson had been assigned the part of the archangel Gabriel. As Jacob watched him recite his lines to the kneeling shepherd, Jacob was struck by how much he reminded him of Benjamin. The same height and thinness. The same slightly awkward limbs that he hadn't yet grown into.

Jacob tried to keep his focus on the boy— the angel—and the story of Christmas. If he so much as looked at the men dressed as shepherds, he might lose his temper. Thinking about Coleman not only robbing an honest man, but then letting an innocent child sit in a jail cell for his crimes all while pretending to be a Christian was more than Jacob could reasonably stand.

He closed his eyes; the congregation would think that he was praying.

Finally, after what seemed like hours, Pastor Ambrose led everyone in a prayer: for the church, for the town, and for the year ahead. Jacob silently added his own petition for Benjamin Wilbourne. He didn't linger a second longer than he needed to, however, certain that God knew what was in his heart.

Even as he was still stepping off the altar, Jacob was pulling the robe up over his head. Bonnie was ready to meet him, handing him both his own coat and the vest borrowed from Coleman. He handed her the robe in turn, the smooth handoff of two people who would make a wonderful team.

"It's here," Bonnie whispered, showing him the spot where the vest was missing a button. "I'll do what I can to distract him, but you need to go."

He nodded, kissing her cheek gratefully with no thought to who could see them or what they would think. He didn't know what he would have done without this woman, and he intended to tell her so.

Just as soon as he saved Benjamin Wilbourne's life.

The agony of having to be polite as he delicately squeezed between groups of churchgoers all standing in the aisles and gossiping, greeting each other, hugging and wishing each other a merry Christmas was excruciating. It took him far longer than he had hoped to reach the front door of the church and head out into the cold evening.

All around him the night was silent, the sun just about set and the chill numbed his cheeks and ears. Jacob was just about to set off at a run, when he was abruptly halted.

A young woman stepped directly into Jacob's path. He couldn't pass her without moving her aside and being rude, and he had never done such a thing to a young woman.

"I'm sorry, I need—"

"Mr. Payne?" she interrupted.

Jacob took a second look at this girl who knew his name. He frowned. "Elizabeth? Miss Towers? Can I—? Is everything all right? Is your family okay?" Jacob hated to be sidetracked but he immediately assumed the worst when Miss Towers would come find him.

"They're fine. Well, all but Benjamin. I need to tell you something."

Anything else out of her mouth would have resulted in a quick dismissal from Jacob, but by simply mentioning Benjamin's name she had his attention.

"Something that you should have told the marshal earlier, maybe?"

He peered down into her face but she kept her eyes lowered. She nodded.

"Well I was just on my way to the courthouse to see if I could maybe convince the judge that Benjamin didn't rob the telegraph office. I don't have a whole lot to go on, though. Is what you have to tell me going to help with that?"

She nodded.

Jacob sighed. Elizabeth Towers was very clearly petrified, and he didn't want to spook her. But at the same time, he should have been at the courthouse hours ago. He looked around, but there was nowhere convenient for him to offer her a seat. He couldn't take this child to a saloon or even the cafe by herself. The only option he had was to stand here on the boardwalk, as the sun was setting, and coax her into trusting him.

He checked his pocket watch again and stifled a groan.

"Miss Towers, I know you care about Benjamin, don't you? I appreciate how much you've already done to help the case, and I'm sure he does too. Why don't you start at the beginning and tell me what you'd like to say? I'm sure whatever it is will be helpful."

"I ..." She spoke so quietly Jacob almost didn't hear her. "I don't want to get in trouble."

"You? Why would you get in trouble? You're such a nice little girl, Miss Towers. I'm sure whatever you have to tell me is pertinent to the case. I know it's scary, but can you tell me? Can you be brave, like Benjamin?"

She squared her shoulders and looked Jacob in the eye again.

"I will. It's this." Another deep breath. "Benjamin was with me when the telegraph office was being robbed. I can speak to his whereabouts that afternoon."

Jacob frowned. "Well ... Miss Towers that's wonderful, but I don't understand why you didn't tell the marshal this earlier. This could change everything. You're sure it was that day? You're absolutely positive?"

She nodded. "I didn't tell the marshal because I was afraid Benjamin would get in trouble for what we were talking about. But now he's in even worse trouble and I know now I shouldn't have hid this. I'll tell the truth if this ever happens again. You see, Mr. Payne, Benjamin was ... Well, rather *I* was fighting with him. He's been a member of our family for as long as I can remember, but now that we're getting older, my folks are talking about me marrying and moving on to some exciting life and Benjamin isn't going to get any of the same privileges I get. It's been weighing on my mind quite a bit these last few months and I wanted to do something about it.

"So, that afternoon in question I had gone to the stock room where he was sorting boxes and I offered him some of my small savings. It's not a lot ... but I think it would be enough for a train ticket somewhere and a little to get him started. I earn a small wage for doing sewing for some of the men who come into our shop. I've been saving up for my trousseau, but I know even with that little pittance I have more than Benjamin does. He's been such a big part of my life, I couldn't let him just ... I would miss him, but I didn't want him to be stuck in that store for the rest of his life. Not if he wanted to be somewhere else.

"I walked in there and I told him what I was offering him and he ..." She sighed, despondent. "He almost yelled at me. He probably would have if my parents hadn't been just on the other side of the door. I didn't mean to insult him. I hadn't thought of it as charity, but he was so mad. I offended him by even offering it. I probably offended him by even having the thought that he needed my money. And ... I don't think Benjamin has ever spoken to me that way. I probably deserved it. I meant well, but I didn't think about what such an offer would do to his masculine pride.

"It was a big fight, Mr. Payne. I've never seen him that angry at anyone. And I cried, and then he was sorry. He almost hugged me, but we both knew that would make Pa angry. It was just … It was a mess all around.

"And I didn't tell the marshal, because I didn't want Benjamin to get in trouble for yelling at me. I didn't want the marshal to know Benjamin had a reason to want cash. I just thought if we told him that he was in the back room all afternoon that would be enough. But I guess it's not."

"No, it's not," Jacob agreed softly. "And Elizabeth, I know it's hard, but I may need you to tell this story to the judge."

She shook her head frantically. "No. I couldn't. Oh, please, Mr. Payne. Please, just tell him yourself. I'll get my father to sign something that says it's true if that will help. I'd rather tell him than a judge."

"Well, we'll see. That might be allowed. But right now, I've got to get to the court. Hopefully I'll be in time to stop Benjamin from being convicted. And you need to come with me."

Tears rolled down Elizabeth's cheeks as the realization of what she had to do hit her. She nodded.

"I'll do my best, Miss Towers. But you do need to come with me. Just in case. If you care about Benjamin."

"I do. I will. I'm sorry."

Jacob nodded. He offered her his arm to escort her the final blocks between the church and the courthouse. Walking as quickly as he could while still being respectful to his guest, Jacob prayed he wouldn't miss it.

CHAPTER FOURTEEN

As Jacob Payne and Elizabeth Towers rounded the corner of the wide street in central Tucson, the warm windows of the courthouse lit their way. Though Jacob had been here a couple times before, he had never been as invested in a case as he was tonight.

"Do you think we're too late?" she asked. "It's Christmas Eve. Everyone is going to want to go home."

"We'll see," he said grimly. "We're doing our best. That's all we can do."

The brick building at the end of the block boasted two large windows on either side of a wide front door. Jacob yanked the door open, ushered the young lady through, before following himself. They hurried through the small foyer into the courtroom itself, trying to stay as quiet as possible. As Jacob entered the courtroom, his eyes were drawn to the witness stand.

U.S. Marshal Owen Santos sat, leaning forward and talking urgently to the judge, an older bald man peering down at the documents on his desk, rather than look at the marshal.

"That's when I decided to arrest Mr. Wilbourne, your Honor," the marshal said. "I felt that all the evidence indicated him to be the most likely culprit."

The judge nodded, reading again one of the papers in his hands. "You say this is similar to one of the buttons that is sold at his place of employment?"

"Yes, your Honor."

"And you think Mr. Wilbourne brought a loose button with him to the robbery?"

"Well." The marshal cleared his throat. "I think it's very possible that a button somehow fell into a cuff or a fold while he was at the general store and then fell out again while he was ... performing the other tasks."

"I see." The judge sighed. "Thank you for your thoroughness, Marshal. Is there anything else I should be aware of?" He glared down at the front row of the courtroom where Benjamin must be sitting.

"Yes!" Jacob shouted from the back of the room. "Yes, sir. Your Honor. Sir, yes, I have some evidence that exonerates Mr. Wilbourne, sir, if you'll allow me."

Jacob rushed up the short aisle until he was standing directly in front of the judge. The older man frowned.

"And you are?"

"This is Mr. Jacob Payne," the marshal interjected. "He's a bounty hunter, but also one of my most trusted lawmen in the territory."

"I see," responded the judge. "And, Marshal, do you think I should listen to this man?"

Jacob looked at Santos, hoping that he hadn't yet offended the lawman in his challenge of him.

He sighed. "Yes, your Honor. I believe that if he's come all the way here on Christmas Eve, Mr. Payne must have something worth reporting."

"Very well. Marshal, you may step down. Mr. Payne, please swear to tell the truth and have a seat."

As soon as the formalities had been taken

care of, Jacob rushed into his report of everything he had learned over the past few days, from the fact that Andrew Coleman encouraged Mr. Wood to leave his shop at midday, to the missing button on his vest, to the fact that no money was found in Benjamin's quarters. He also told the judge about the fight that the young man and Miss Towers had had, though he tried to brush over that as quickly as possible so as to not embarrass the young lady.

Throughout Jacob's recitation of the facts, he kept glancing between the marshal and the judge, watching each of their expressions for clues that he was being believed. He didn't dare look at Benjamin, for fear that he was going to let the poor kid down.

Once he was finished, Jacob still sat forward, his hands resting on his knees, Coleman's vest having already been handed over to the judge to be grouped with the rest of the evidence.

"And so, your Honor, I believe the true culprit may still be at the church or near to it. If you two both approve, I'm happy to go apprehend the real suspect and Mr. Wilbourne here can be free to go."

The judge didn't look at him. He was

comparing the button found at the scene to the buttons still sewn on to the vest.

"You know ... It does seem as though this button found is more worn than a new one would be. I think you make good points, Mr. Payne. But I can't just declare this Coleman character guilty instead of Mr. Wilbourne. He deserves to be present for his own trial after all."

"Of course, your Honor. I understand. Of course. I just— It was most important to me that an innocent man not be convicted."

"Hrmph," the judge grunted. "In my experience, few fifteen-year-old boys are completely innocent of everything. But ..." He looked down to where the accused sat, handcuffed in the front row of the court room.

For the first time since entering the building, Jacob permitted himself a look at Benjamin. He seemed to be cautiously relieved; he sat up straighter, though he made no move to get up. The young man knew his place before even being stuck in a jail cell, and it was likely that the events of the week had cured him of any desire to break the law at all.

The judge pulled out his pocket watch.

"Very well then," he said slowly. "Mr. Payne, I applaud your efforts to find the truth. It is my belief that justice has been served tonight. I declare Mr. Benjamin Wilbourne not guilty of the crime of robbery."

Jacob let out a long sigh of relief.

"Marshal, it may not be exactly my place to say, but I encourage you look into this Coleman character for the crime. Given the late hour, I will not be staying to try another case, but any additional inmates can wait their turn in a jail cell until the circuit brings me back to Tucson."

Jacob chanced a look at the marshal. He grinned and nodded.

"Go ahead, Payne. I'll meet you at the jail."

Jacob went. He didn't need to be told twice. He darted down the aisle of the courthouse at a speed he wished he could have taken in the church. In the foyer, he slowed only enough to tell Miss Towers that her testimony wasn't needed. That Benjamin should be free soon to see her home. And thank her.

But then he was out the door.

Jacob ran. He ran down the dark, empty streets of Tucson. Nearly all the citizens of the town were home on this night before Christmas. As Jacob cut down a street and passed a few homes, he heard the plinking of piano and the sweet tones of a family singing "Stille Nacht" in the original German. The bounty hunter felt a warm surge of home and family and love speed him on toward the church, toward where he hoped to find the thief.

As with every other outlaw that Jacob had apprehended, this one reeked of arrogance and the certainty that he wouldn't be caught. And Jacob knew that was precisely the circumstance that would allow him to seize the man.

The bounty hunter rounded the final corner and stopped in his tracks. The church was dark and closed. Everyone had left the church in the short time Jacob had been gone. It's not as though he had expected anyone to wait for him to come back and arrest them, but Jacob was surprised briefly by the total absence of people.

He would have to find Coleman another way.

It was Christmas Eve. Coleman wasn't going to get a stagecoach out of town for at least a couple days. That left only one other option: the Golden Saddle Saloon.

If he was wrong about this, Jacob didn't know where to try next, so he went full bore back down the street toward the only establishment in town that seemed to have people.

As with the courthouse only an hour or so earlier, the warm, lit windows of the saloon drew Jacob in. From the outside, judging by the stream of traffic through the door, it seemed as though every man in Tucson who didn't have a family—that is, most of them—was in the saloon that evening. Jacob would probably find his quarry there, though actually locating him in the crowd might be difficult.

Jacob managed to slip through the door into the Golden Saddle Saloon, but could advance no further. The crowd of men around the bar was at least ten men deep. Though the bounty hunter wasn't there for a beer, he still couldn't find a way past all the men that were.

His height, however, gave him an advantage. It was no trouble at all for Jacob to spot his prey sitting near the back of the room with Clifford Pierce and another couple familiar faces. All the men seemed jovial and relaxed, never thinking for a second their lives were about to change.

Focused on his destination, Jacob elbowed his way through the crowd toward Coleman. His eyes never left the other man's face and he recognized the exact moment that he realized Jacob was coming for him.

There was a brief lull, a small pause as the thief seemed to debate how to handle the situation. He could feign ignorance or he could run.

Coleman chose to run.

Unfortunately for him, there was nowhere to run.

He had only managed to push away from the table and dive into another group of men standing nearby when Jacob caught up with him. Laying both hands on the man's shoulders, Jacob snarled, "Marshal Santos needs to see you. Now."

CHAPTER FIFTEEN

Handing Andrew Coleman over to U.S. Marshal Owen Santos was one of the most satisfying things Jacob had done in a while. True, it wasn't quite the same thing as a conviction from the judge, but the fact that the real thief was in custody and Benjamin Wilbourne was not was enough for Jacob.

He had been so focused on freeing the young man that Jacob hadn't had much chance to think about the holiday the following day or how he would spend it. Even his time as Joseph during the Nativity play was full of thoughts of clues and crimes.

But now, as the sun rose on Christmas Day, Jacob found himself with a day empty of responsibilities or appointments.

And he knew there was only one way he wanted to spend it.

It wouldn't be the first time he made his way over to Bonnie Loft's boarding house the first thing in the morning, but he didn't think her landlady Mrs. Withers would be any happier to see him this day than any previous.

But, there was no help for it. Jacob wanted to see Bonnie. He needed to see her. He had done enough thinking about it and now it was time to take action. What better day than Christmas Day to tell someone how he felt about her?

It was only after knocking on the door to the boarding house that Jacob realized he might be interrupting a big holiday breakfast or some other tradition. He hadn't yet lived in the Arizona Territory the previous December; he didn't quite know what to expect from the settlers that had left all the trappings and tradition of the east coast to come to the wild western frontier.

He didn't get far in these thoughts before the door opened and the very woman he was looking for stood before him.

"Bonnie," he said, almost breathlessly. She looked stunning—a deep green dress that both showed off her alabaster complexion and called to mind the home and holiday that most people were celebrating that day. "Is this a bad time?"

She smiled at him, as though she had been expecting his visit. "Of course not."

"Can you ... Would you please take a walk with me?" He gestured out into the cold December sunshine. Almost no one was out in the town this early on Christmas Day; they could have virtual privacy.

"Wait here. One moment." She closed the door gently, leaving him on the front porch for just a few minutes before reemerging with cloak and muff to keep her warm while outdoors.

Jacob offered his arm, thinking how lucky he was to have met her, how grateful he was that she seemed to care for him.

As they walked—Jacob realized he had subconsciously steered them toward the Everlasting Hope Church—Bonnie pressed him with questions of the night before. The last she had seen of him, Jacob had been darting off to the marshal's office carrying Coleman's vest. He was happy to fill her in on the results of their investigation.

"Oh, I'm so glad," Bonnie exclaimed when she learned that her discovery of the missing button had so helped. "I couldn't stop thinking about that poor boy last night, thinking about him sitting in a cold jail cell on Christmas Eve."

"Nope, he got to go home. I don't know how warm it was, but at least it was his own bed. And Coleman was the one sitting in jail."

"I'm so happy to hear that."

The couple found themselves on the road in front of their church. Jacob looked up at the stark white building against the clear blue sky and made his decision. He gently guided Bonnie up the front path of the church to the geraniums that had been planted on either side of the front door. The deep pink blooms sprinkled here and there lent a softness and welcoming air to the garden.

Bonnie continued, "No one should be alone on Christmas, though. Maybe we should take Mr. Coleman a piece of pie."

"Maybe," Jacob said noncommittally. "I'm just grateful to not be alone myself this Christmas. Last year was particularly hard for me; this year is much different."

"Oh yes, weren't you traveling out west at this time last year?"

Jacob nodded. "The trip out wasn't so bad, but ... well, this year is different. I hope you know how much you have to do with that."

He turned to face Bonnie, and she

removed one hand from her fur muff to be held in his. Looking down into her dark eyes, Jacob felt instinctively that they understood each other.

"Bonnie, I want to say something. About how much this last year has meant to me."

"All right." Her warm smile all but made his heart burst with love and pride.

"I truly believe that every step on each of our paths has led us to each other, to this moment. If I had stayed in the New Mexico Territory, or if you had married the fellow back east your mother wanted you to. Even if I hadn't been craving a pork chop that first day I walked into the San Xavier Cafe and met you for the first time."

She laughed at the memory.

"Every one of those choices has brought us into each other's lives and has showed me your character, and hopefully you mine. You make me want to be the best man I can be. Every one of those choices displayed for me exactly how well you would fit with me and how happy we could be together.

"Bonnie Loft, I want to come home to you every night. I want you to be by my side through the victories and the struggles. There is nothing I would rather do with the rest of my life than spend it with you. I love you. Will you marry me?"

She looked down, and for the briefest moment Jacob wondered if he had misjudged her attachment to him.

But the pure expression of adoration that she offered him when she looked up told Jacob everything he needed to know.

"Yes," she said softly. "Of course, I will. I am so happy to be your wife."

He took her in his arms and kissed her, long and luxuriously, pulling her tightly and taking as much time as he thought he could get away with. True, they had kissed before, but not like this. Not with this love and promise of a lifetime between them.

When he finally pulled away, Bonnie could not stop smiling. She laughed a little with the joy of it.

"Now," she said, tucking her hand back into his arm, "come back home with me and share in a Christmas dinner. Mrs. Withers won't be happy, but I don't want to spend any other holidays without you."

Jacob kissed her again, before leading her out of the church yard, back home and toward their life together.

Lonesome Trail

Before Jacob Payne arrived in the Arizona Territory, before he was a bounty hunter, before he learned how to survive in the desert, he had to travel west. Innocents in trouble, quirky characters and life-threatening peril  are along every mile as he passed from Virginia through Texas to the desert of Arizona.

When Jacob comes across a family that has fallen victim to horse thieves, he can't just ride on and leave them to his fate. He's not yet a bounty hunter, but Jacob Payne can still hunt down the evil-doers. Tucson will be waiting for him once he brings these men to justice.

Sign-up to download this prequel story for free from my website:

http://atbutler.com/jp-free

ALSO BY A.T. BUTLER

Hawke's Revenge

Loyalty's Price

ABOUT THE AUTHOR

I grew up in the southwest—California Missions, snakes and constant threat of drought weaving the backdrop of my childhood.

But it wasn't until I moved to Texas a few years ago that the magic and mythology of the American West began to seep into my soul.

I'd love to write western adventures for a long time. ...

If you enjoyed this book, a review on your favorite retailer would be greatly appreciated.

- A

Created with Vellum